The World's MOST DANGEROUS Jobs

Test Pilots

By Antony Loveless

CRABTREE
Publishing Company
www.crabtreebooks.com

The World's MOST DANGEROUS Jobs

Editors: Mark Sachner, Adrianna Morganelli
Editorial director: Kathy Middleton
Proofreader: Redbud Editorial
Production coordinator: Margaret Salter
Prepress technician: Margaret Salter
Project director: Ruth Owen
Designer: Elaine Wilkinson
Cover design: Alix Wood

Photo credits:
Crown Copyright: pages 1, 6, 7, 12, 14–15
Department of Defense: cover (top), pages 5, 8, 9, 22–23, 25, 27
Getty Images: AFP: page 21
Antony Loveless: cover (bottom), pages 17, 18, 19, 28–29
Rob Schenk: page 10

COVER STORY

◄ **COVER (top) – An F-35 Lightning II fighter jet, also known as the Joint Strike Fighter, on a test flight.**

◄ **COVER (bottom) – A test pilot inside a Royal Air Force (RAF) Tornado F-3 fighter jet.**

PAGE 1 – Empire Test Pilot School's Class of 2006 outside the Officers Mess. The class is made up of top class pilots from around the world.

Library and Archives Canada Cataloguing in Publication

Loveless, Antony
    Test pilots / Antony Loveless.

(The world's most dangerous jobs)
Includes index.
ISBN 978-0-7787-5099-4 (bound).--ISBN 978-0-7787-5113-7 (pbk)

    1. Test pilots--Juvenile literature. 2. Air pilots, Military--Juvenile
literature. 3. Airplanes--Flight testing--Juvenile literature. I. Title.
II. Series: World's most dangerous jobs

TL671.7.L69 2009   j629.134'53   C2009-903382-8

Library of Congress Cataloging-in-Publication Data

Loveless, Antony.
    Test pilots / Antony Loveless.
        p. cm. -- (The world's most dangerous jobs)
    Includes index.
    ISBN 978-0-7787-5099-4 (reinforced lib. bdg. : alk. paper)
    -- ISBN 978-0-7787-5113-7 (pbk. : alk. paper)
    1. Test pilots--Juvenile literature. 2. Air pilots--Juvenile literature.
3. Airplanes--Flight testing--Juvenile literature. 4. Air pilots, Military--
Juvenile literature. I. Title. II. Series.

    TL671.7.L68 2009
    629.13--dc22

                                            2009022042

Published by CRABTREE PUBLISHING COMPANY in 2010

Copyright © 2010 Ruby Tuesday Books Ltd

Published in Canada
Crabtree Publishing
616 Welland Ave.
St. Catharines, ON
L2M 5V6

Published in the United States
Crabtree Publishing
PMB16A
350 Fifth Ave., Suite 3308
New York, NY 10118

Published in the United Kingdom
Crabtree Publishing
Lorna House, Suite 3.03, Lorna Road
Hove, East Sussex, UK
BN3 3EL

Published in Australia
Crabtree Publishing
386 Mt. Alexander Rd.
Ascot Vale (Melbourne)
VIC 3032

CONTENTS

TEST PILOT

In today's world, most people do not take part in dangerous activities during their day at work. They sit at desks in offices, or they work in shops and factories. For some people, however, facing danger is very much a part of their working life.

The job of a test pilot is one of the most demanding and dangerous in the world of aviation.

Test pilots are **aviators** who specialize in a particularly risky form of flying. When new aircraft are introduced, or existing aircraft designs are improved or changed, it's the job of a test pilot to fly the aircraft and report back on how it handles.

It might seem that the test pilot's world is one of daredevils, excitement, and **adrenaline**. The reality is that test pilots must be highly professional, precise, and scientific in everything they do.

Test pilots do not spend all their time flying. Most of their time is spent on the ground working on scientific **equations,** evaluating flight test results, and writing long, technical reports.

Ultimately, their job is to determine if the planes they test can safely do what they were designed to do—before the rest of the flying world takes those planes into the air.

▼ An F-35 Lightning II fighter jet on a test flight.
The plane is also known as the Joint Strike Fighter.

Test pilots are generally military pilots.
Some civilian pilots—those trained by commercial airlines—
do become test pilots, too. A test pilot's work combines flying
with engineering and aeronautics—the science of flying.

WHAT DO TEST PILOTS DO?

There are several different types of test pilots, and each type tests a different kind of aircraft. Experimental and engineering test pilots fly newly-designed aircraft. The test pilots fly the new aircraft to be sure that they operate according to their original design.

Another type of test pilot, production test pilots, test-fly every new aircraft as it comes off the assembly line in the manufacturer's factory. Airline test pilots test-fly commercial airliners after major overhauls. They also test new airliners when they are delivered from the manufacturer.

Aircraft are allowed to fly only if they are constructed within tightly controlled design standards and guidelines. Every new fuel tank—or missile or bomb, if the aircraft is a military plane—that is added to an existing design affects how the aircraft will handle. Before a new design can be approved, test pilots must report back on how the aircraft will be affected by that design.

▲ An Apache AH-1 helicopter test fires flares. These are used to divert the path of heat-seeking missiles by presenting a hotter target than anything on the aircraft.

▶ All weapons have to be tested on aircraft to examine how they affect the handling of the aircraft. Here, a Merlin helicopter test-drops a torpedo into the sea during the weapon's evaluation stage.

"Every last detail about how the aircraft flies must be recorded and checked so that nothing unexpected can go wrong when it's eventually used to fly missions or passengers.

The way it flies must be closely scrutinized. We must be totally aware of every detail of the test flight. We'll ensure that we face every potentially problematic situation that might arise, but in a controlled and monitored environment. That way, in the heat of battle or when an emergency occurs (on a commercial airliner), there is no chance of a minor technical flaw resulting in an operational failure that actually costs lives."

Roger, Former United Kingdom Royal Air Force (RAF) and Boeing Test Pilot

THE DANGERS

All new aircraft begin life as two-dimensional (2D) drawings. Then engineers assess their **aerodynamic** efficiency using three-dimensional (3D) scale models tested in **wind tunnels**. The test pilots then spend many hours in a flight simulator that recreates many conditions of flight without the risks.

Eventually, once the first life-size test aircraft is built, it is the test pilot's job to take the new design into the air for the first time.

All flying is risky, but pilots normally fly within strict safety limits. But who makes the rules about each aircraft's limits? Who knows what happens if you fly outside the limits? Test pilots do, and that's why their job is so dangerous. A test pilot pushes an aircraft up to and beyond its limits.

The **F-22 Raptor** is a modern fighter jet in service with a number of United States Air Force (USAF) units. Like all aircraft, it still undergoes test-flying when modifications are added. In March 2009, an F-22 crashed in California during a flight test. The test pilot, David Cooley, was killed. Cooley was an experienced test pilot with 21 years of flying experience. David Cooley's story goes to show that experience and a long career are no guarantee of survival in the world of the test pilot.

◄ Test pilots Captain Charles E. "Chuck" Yeager (left) and Captain Jackie L. Ridley. In 1947, Yeager became the first pilot to travel faster than the speed of sound (770 mph/1,240 km/h). He was flying the Bell X-1 (pictured) at an altitude of 45,000 feet (13,700 meters).

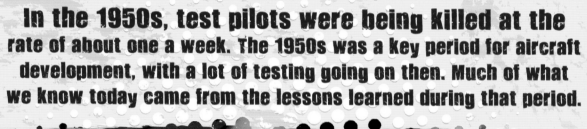

In the 1950s, test pilots were being killed at the rate of about one a week. The 1950s was a key period for aircraft development, with a lot of testing going on then. Much of what we know today came from the lessons learned during that period.

▲ A test pilot connects the oxygen hose to his helmet mask before taking off on a flight test in an F-16 Fighting Falcon.

▲ An F-16 Fighting Falcon test pilot assigned to the United States Air Force's (USAF's) 85th Test and Evaluation Squadron watches his AGM-88 High-Speed Anti-Radiation Missile (HARM) race past the cockpit after firing during a test mission.

WHO CAN BECOME A TEST PILOT?

Most test pilots are well educated and have a history of military flying.

Test pilots usually have one or two degrees in the field of engineering. They must also have operational experience (real-life flying experience) of flying helicopters, fighter jets, or large multi-engine aircraft, such as airliners. A test pilot recruit may have as many as 5,000 flying hours.

Test pilots need to have a good understanding of what makes planes fly the way they do. They must have excellent powers of observation and the ability to reason—to explain things and figure out problems. Test pilots must also have strong analytical skills and be able to explain their findings clearly to those they report to. This ensures that good designs make it into service and bad ones don't!

Air forces select experienced pilots from their ranks who appear to have the unique qualities required for the job of test pilot. They then send them for a year of specialized training at a test pilot school.

Civilian test pilots work for airline manufacturers such as Airbus and Boeing.

▼ The Empire Test Pilot School's Hawk T1 in a dive while on a test flight with a student.

"Students taking the ETPS course are experienced operational pilots from front-line squadrons with an above average flying ability. As they work through the ETPS curriculum, they can expect to fly as many as 30 different aircraft types."

James, UK Royal Air Force (RAF) Instructor at the Empire Test Pilot School

▲ Test pilots taking the Empire Test Pilot School's first course, which ran from April 1943 to January 1944.

EMPIRE TEST PILOT SCHOOL

There are four military and two civilian test pilot schools in Europe and the United States. Some air forces send their students to all the schools in order to gain the broadest range of flight test expertise.

The Empire Test Pilot School in the United Kingdom was formed in 1942. It was the first test pilot school anywhere in the world. Today, test pilot candidates from air forces around the world train at ETPS.

The courses at ETPS last for 11 months. They are very hard work and unforgiving—only the very best will make it through. On average, each course produces just nine fully trained test pilots.

"Extensive use is made of the school's unique Hawk T1. This plane has been modified to be used as an 'Advanced Stability Training and Research Aircraft.' The front cockpit is effectively converted into a flight simulator. The instructor in the rear cockpit can modify the flight characteristics to act like almost any fast jet for the student in the front. The **center of gravity**, performance, and handling of the Hawk T1 can all be adjusted. So, for the student 'flying' the Hawk T1 it can be made to react and feel like, for example, an F-16 fighter jet or the F-35 Lightning II."

James, Royal Air Force (RAF) Instructor at the Empire Test Pilot School

THE TEST FACTORY

It's not easy to secure a place in a course at the Empire Test Pilot School. The school generally interviews three times the number of students it has places for.

Students from the United Kingdom and United States are accepted onto the ETPS courses with a specific test pilot job waiting for them when they graduate. If they pass the ETPS course, the newly qualified test pilots will be deployed for a three-year tour of duty as part of the test squadron at MOD Boscombe Down—the test center alongside the ETPS school. The test center is known as "The Test Factory."

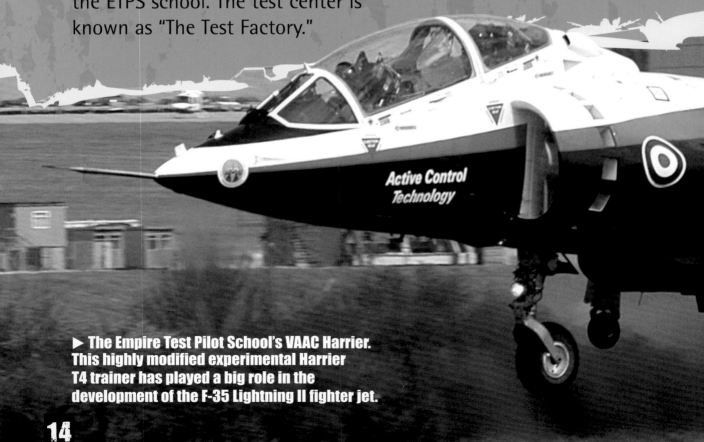

▶ The Empire Test Pilot School's VAAC Harrier. This highly modified experimental Harrier T4 trainer has played a big role in the development of the F-35 Lightning II fighter jet.

"The ETPS course teaches students how to turn their opinions about an aircraft into a watertight argument that can be communicated to others.

Test flights of one to two hours might take a day to plan. The student test pilots will consult with engineers and the design team to establish specific tasks and requirements for each sortie, or test flight. At the end of each sortie they are expected to write a lengthy report on the capabilities and characteristics of the aircraft flown. They must also deliver a presentation to a board of senior officers, then take questions for over an hour. It's a punishing workload."

James, RAF Instructor at the Empire Test Pilot School

FLIGHT SIMULATORS

When test pilots take a new plane into the air for the first time, they will be very familiar with the aircraft's cockpit. This is thanks to an extraordinary invention—the full motion flight simulator.

Carl is a senior captain with British Airways and a qualified simulator instructor with the airline. Here is what he says:

"These state-of-the-art machines have as much in common with videogame-based flight simulators as a Ferrari F430 does to a Matchbox toy Ferrari! A trainee airline pilot can do all his or her training in one of these. The first time they take the controls of a real plane will be when they have passengers in the back. If you're worried by that, you shouldn't be—these machines are incredible!

Simulator cockpits are identical to the real thing in every way. They have all the same instruments, buttons, levers, switches, and pedals. They move in three dimensions to exactly replicate the feel of the real thing. All the sounds, alarms, and views through the screen are spot on. This level of realism doesn't come cheap, however—each simulator costs around $22 million."

▶ **Final approach at New York's JFK airport in a Boeing 777. Although it looks like the real thing, this picture was taken inside a Boeing 777 full motion simulator.**

A simulator is kept in a lab-like room.
It is mounted on hydraulic legs that give the simulator
movement. The simulator's controls are linked to massive
computers that can generate all the situations
that a real aircraft might experience.

During flight testing, commercial airliners are stripped down to the metal inside. They are filled with scientific equipment that measure and record everything that happens on the flight for analysis.

▲ The interior of an Airbus A380 during flight testing.

AIRBUS A380

The Airbus A380 is the world's largest passenger airliner. It is also the world's most recently introduced commercial aircraft.

The aircraft is known by its nickname—"Superjumbo." It features two decks, and its upper deck extends along almost the entire length of the fuselage.

The A380 can accommodate 525 passengers in a standard three-class layout—economy class, business class, and first class. If configured (set up) just for economy class, it can carry up to 853 passengers.

Five Airbus A380s were built for testing purposes. The first test plane, serial number MSN001, made its first flight on April 27, 2005.

The plane was piloted by Airbus's chief test pilot, Jacques Rosay. With a crew of five onboard, Rosay took off from Toulouse in France on a four-hour test flight.

▲ An Airbus A380 takes off on a test flight during the testing and evaluation stage of its design.

TESTING THE AIRBUS A380

Following its maiden, or first, flight in April 2005, the A380 underwent a series of important flight tests. The tests were conducted by a team of test pilots, each responsible for one aspect of the flight.

The A380 flew transatlantic test flights. It was also tested at high-altitude airports and in cold-weather destinations. All these test flights were successful.

On February 14, 2006, the A380 failed its first test. An aircraft's wings are what keep it in the air. The A380's wings needed to be able to carry 50 percent more weight than the plane's normal weight when loaded. In the tests, the wings only reached 45 percent. This is a good example of what test pilots do. Using data from the failed test, Airbus was able to make amendments to the A380's design.

On March 26, 2006, the A380 underwent one of its final, and perhaps one of the most important, tests—evacuation certification. Certification standards required that it must be possible to evacuate the plane in 90 seconds or less. With eight of its 16 exits blocked, 853 passengers and 20 crew members managed to "escape" from the Airbus A380 in 78 seconds.

Three days later, the A380 received European Aviation Safety Agency (EASA) and United States Federal Aviation Administration (FAA) approval to carry up to 853 passengers. Test-flying for the A380 was complete.

Test pilot Jacques Rosay found the A380 so easy to handle on its first flight that he later said it had been "like handling a bicycle."

▶ Test pilot Captain Jean-Michel Roy in the cockpit of the Airbus A380.

F-35 LIGHTNING II

The F-35 Lightning II (or Joint Strike Fighter), which is currently in development, will be the most up-to-date and efficient fighter jet in the world. Lockheed Martin, the F-35's manufacturer, will begin delivery to the United States Air Force (USAF) and U.K. Royal Air Force (RAF) in 2012.

The F-35 can take off from just a few yards of runway and land vertically. It does this by using a huge fan that provides 20,000 pounds (9,070 kilograms) of thrust. This enables the plane to hover before touching down.

The F-35 is being developed as a replacement for the **Harrier jump jet**. The jet has all the maneuverability of the Harrier but with a top speed of 1,200 mph (1,930 km/h)—twice the speed of the Harrier!

The F-35 uses **stealth** techniques to evade **radar**. Any sharp angles on the plane's airframe (its body and wings) have been eliminated wherever possible. This gives the F-35 an amazing quality—it will be as difficult to spot using radar as a steel golf ball in the sky.

Lockheed Martin chief test pilot Jon Beesley has flown in the development phase of every operational USAF stealth aircraft. In his current role, he is bringing together all of his abilities and experience to get the F-35 into the air. So far, he has logged hundreds of hours in F-35 simulators.

> " I spend a great deal of time in meetings, working with the engineers on every aspect of how the landing gear works, how the flight control works, how the airplane flies, how the displays work, how the helmet works, writing the flight manual—all that stuff. "
>
> Jon Beesley, Lockheed Martin Chief Test Pilot

◄ Test pilot Jon Beesley testing the new F-35 Lightning II. This new fighter-bomber has the very latest in Star Wars-style technology and the most powerful fighter jet engine ever built.

TESTING F-35S

F-35 pilots will fly the aircraft through a combination of voice commands and touchscreen controls.

Rather than evolving the F-35 from previous designs, engineers decided to start with a clean sheet of paper. Existing cockpits present a pilot with lots of instruments that show all the plane's systems and situations all of the time. In the F-35, engineers give priority just to the information that the pilot needs at any precise moment.

Gone are the dials and switches—they have all been replaced with a single 20-inch- (60-centimeter-) wide, LCD, touchscreen color display. Pilots will be able to customize the screen to only display the instruments they want to see at any particular time.

Existing fighter jets have a Head-Up Display (HUD) system. This projects key flight and weapons information onto a lens fixed to the top of the instrument console in the pilot's direct line of sight.

" The F-35 introduces a completely new system called a Helmet-Mounted Display (HMD). This allows the helmet to project the information directly onto the pilot's visor. The pilot can see the information wherever he or she looks. F-35 pilots will be able to look in different directions to maintain situational awareness outside the cockpit, while seeing key tactical and flight information in their line of sight. The pilot can also launch weapons simply by looking at targets. "

Jon Beesley, Lockheed Martin Chief Test Pilot

The F-35's onboard software will diagnose mechanical problems and assess battle damage. It will then radio instructions ahead to ground crews.

Virtual representation of the 3D display seen by the pilot through the visor

Touchscreen display

▲ F-35 cockpit at dusk with virtual projection of Helmet Mounted Display.

A DAY IN THE LIFE

New aircraft, such as the F-35, are often a joint project between two or more countries. This means air force test pilots travel a great deal in their job.

"I spend some of my time in the cockpit conducting flight tests. Although it's not terribly physical, there is a considerable amount of stress involved. Pushing an aircraft to its maximum performance abilities during its developmental stages can be dangerous. You have to be constantly aware.

I assess aircraft for their structural integrity—how well the fuselage withstands the stresses placed upon it. I also test-fly them for performance, handling, reliability, and suitability for the role they will be used for.

Flight tests represent the smallest portion of my time, though. I spend most of my working day in the office planning test procedures or assessing the results of those I've already undertaken. We're required to provide highly technical written and oral (spoken) reports on flight experiences. We must also recommend ways to fix any problems.

A lot of each day is spent writing lengthy, detailed reports, and some of it is even spent getting involved with mathematical formulas and equations—it's all a far cry from flying a plane."

James, United States Air Force (USAF) Test Pilot

"It's a pretty unique lifestyle! We combine fighter pilot-style flying, with lots of travel, presentations to officers way above our own rank, and lots of academic and highly technical work."

Edward, Royal Navy Test Pilot

▶ Test-flying a USAF F-22 Raptor. Test pilots are trained to expect the unexpected as an aircraft is tested to the limits of its capabilities.

TEST-FLYING CONCORDE

On July 25, 2000, an Air France Concorde, Flight 4590 to New York, crashed shortly after takeoff from Paris. All 100 passengers and nine crew onboard the flight, as well as four people on the ground, were killed.

A few days after the crash, all Concordes were grounded.

An investigation discovered that a piece of debris had punctured one of the Concorde's tires. The tire exploded and broke an electrical cable before hitting the fuel tank. This caused a fuel leak that was ignited by sparks from the electrical cables. A number of modifications were made, including more secure electrical controls and an armor lining on the fuel tanks.

◀ Chief Concorde test pilot Captain Mike Bannister at the controls of the Concorde. The plane is traveling at 1,300 mph (2,090 km/h) at 50,000 feet (15,240 m), somewhere over the Atlantic.

"I was involved in getting Concorde back in the air as safely as possible. Concorde's manufacturers, Airbus U.K., and I designed the specifics for the test flight and then practiced them in our flight simulator.

We had to test the effect on fuel capacity of the additional weight of the new fuel-tank lining and electrical wiring armor. We had already calculated this but needed to check it in practice. When Concorde flew she got very warm. In fact, the fuselage would stretch by six to 10 inches (15 to 25 cm) when warm. Any modifications to the plane might affect the stretching.

The plane performed exceptionally well. Early indications were that our calculations on the ground were rather conservative (too careful). The increase in the aircraft's weight was offset by a new interior and new lighter tires. There was no difference in the way the aircraft handled.

In general terms, it performed brilliantly. It felt fantastic to be flying again. I first flew Concorde in 1977, but that test flight was the highlight of my career."

Captain Mike Bannister, Chief Concorde Test Pilot, British Airways

▼ **Before the Concorde was retired, it flew between London and New York. Flying at Mach 2—twice the speed of sound—it was capable of making the flight in just under three hours.**

G-BOAF

IT'S A FACT!

Test pilot William C. Ocker was known as the father of "Blind Flying." He flew from Brooks Field, San Antonio, Texas, to March Field, California, in a covered cockpit to prove that a plane's instruments could be more reliable than a pilot's natural senses.

Brian Trubshaw was the chief British test pilot on Concorde. The aircraft was developed by the British and French governments. In April 1969, Trubshaw became the first pilot to fly the British-assembled Concorde.

Hanna Reitsch was a German test pilot who served as Adolf Hitler's personal pilot during World War II. She was the first female pilot to fly a helicopter; fly a rocket plane and fly a jet fighter.

Captain Eric "Winkle" Brown is a former Royal Navy officer and test pilot. He is listed in the Guinness Book of World Records as having flown more aircraft types – 487 – than any other pilot in the world.

American Neil Armstrong was a test pilot at the National Advisory Committee for Aeronautics (NACA) High-Speed Flight Station in the 1950s. He flew over 900 flights in a variety of aircraft. Armstrong later became famous as the first person to set foot on the Moon.

Test Pilots online
www.qinetiq.com/home_etps.html
www.navair.navy.mil/USNTPS/

GLOSSARY

adrenaline A substance produced in the body in response to excitement. Adrenaline makes the heart beat faster.

aerodynamic Having to do with aerodynamics, which is the study of the relationship between air and solid objects moving through it.

altitude Height of a thing above a certain level, especially above sea level or above Earth's surface.

aviator Another word for "pilot."

center of gravity This is the point in an object around which its mass is evenly distributed. Imagine a see-saw—its center of gravity is in the middle, as any weight at either end will cause it to lose balance. It's a key concept within aviation because it affects an aircraft's handling. As fuel burns, the aircraft becomes lighter, which affects its handling and balance.

civilian A person who is not in a branch of the military, such as the army, air force, or navy.

equation A mathematical calculation.

F-16 Fighting Falcon A highly maneuverable single-seat, multi-role fighter aircraft designed and produced by the United States. It is in service with the United States Air Force (USAF). With a top speed of 1,500 mph (2,400 km/h), it is capable of flying above 50,000 feet (15,240 meters).

F-22 Raptor The F-22 Raptor is a fighter jet in service with the United States Air Force (USAF). It is equipped for attack in the air and for bombing targets on the ground. It can fly at over 1,500 mph (2,400 km/h).

harrier jump jet A fighter jet that can make vertical takeoffs and landings. It can also stop dead in midair, fly backward and sideways, and also hover in the air like a helicopter.

radar A way of detecting distant objects. Radar can determine an object's position and speed by sending radio waves that reflect off the object's surface.

stealth Having to do with technology that makes aircraft almost invisible to radar. This is done with panels that absorb rather than reflect radar waves.

wind tunnel A tubular chamber in which a steady current of air can be maintained at a controlled speed. It is equipped with devices for measuring and recording forces on scale models of complete aircraft or, sometimes, on actual full-scale aircraft.

INDEX

Printed in the USA—BG